S. ESCOBAR

A Song Beyond Walls

S. Escobar
Copyright © 2020

All rights reserved. No part of this publication may be reproduced, distributed, or transmitted in any form or by any means, including photocopying, recording, or other electronic or mechanical methods, without the prior written permission of the publisher, except in the case of brief quotations embodied in critical reviews and certain other noncommercial uses permitted by copyright law.

This novel is entirely a work of fiction. The names, characters and incidents portrayed in it are the work of the author's imagination. Any resemblance to actual persons, living or dead, events or localities is entirely coincidental.

Cover design and interior illustrations by Daniela Coronado

ISBN 978-1-7357380-2-4 (paperback)
ISBN 978-1-7357380-1-7 (e-book)

Printed in USA

For the one I call "home"

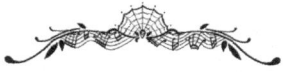

The Unraveled

I remember Time. I remember how clocks would measure Time with gears that grinded so that hands could turn, and that consequential *click* that was a reminder of its passing. I used to have a clock here—a beautiful mahogany one that chimed in the parlor. But it was one of the first things taken . . . along with the silver, all the good chairs, and anything else that held value. All I've been left with are the sofas that have crumbled under their own weight and a broken piano I once loved to play. I'm sure it would still make music if only I could touch it.

Time, though. I remember the circle of it—how the hours pass and begin again with a new day. But I am no longer bound to that single dimension. The circle became to me a sphere. What once I thought were minutes now hold their own pocket in the infinite Great Space, and in that space I linger, dissipated like a gas, spread almost to nonexistence. Purpose and reason are no longer relevant to me, but I can recall what it felt like to be possessed by the illusions of the physical world. Illusions of rules, of beauty, of worth.

The living are so confined by barriers, most of which are of their own imagining. I have seen a few of them—the living—come here into my dwelling. Their shoes groan on the wooden floorboards, leaving shapes upon the dust; their eyes glance around at the peeling wallpaper, the circle of ceiling from where the missing chandelier had been torn, and how still-more dust has caked every surface like snow. They wonder what happened here . . . why such a dismal place has become of what had once, surely, been a gleaming and merry house. I can only assume they return to wherever they came from and speak to others of what they have seen here . . . what they have judged. How this house is not clean and beautiful anymore; how it is too much work to repair. How it frightens them, a little, to feel like they are being watched.

To think I had once been bound by flesh and cloth like them . . . to have had a body—a *shape*—feet that planted upon the ground, hands that could reach out for whatever I wanted to touch. Such boundaries . . . such limits I was imprisoned by, that even my own corset was a cage. But if it was possible for me to want, in this dissipated form in which I am now, I would want it again. When I first became unraveled—like a cloth undone of its threads—and lost without form in this Great Space, I was terrified. I much preferred being snug in a single, moveable body.

How long since my unraveling? The sun rises and falls in an incomprehensible blur. It could have been hours; it could have been a thousand years. Fashions have changed, that much I have been able to tell by those few who have come by here to evaluate my home. Their physical world is a fog to me once they cross beyond the front door, but I can feel that much has changed in it. The Great Space has vibrated with movement, knowledge, technology, growth, and destruction. Now, if only one of the living would stay here longer, I could study them. I have many questions.

I did not have to wait for this, however. For at some point in Time—I cannot tell when, as I am unbound to any measure of it—the door opened again and in walked a man with a case hanging from each hand. He stepped in and looked about the space as all the others had done but with an expression that was different than theirs had been. He looked . . . *intrigued* . . . if I remember that expression properly. His first thought was not what the place would look like if it was cleaned of all its dust and made to sparkle again, but how grand the place was already.

His dress was much different from when I was alive; it was even different from the men's before him. This man wore simpler clothes with less fastenings: a rough-looking three-piece tweed suit and a hat that looked almost squashed over his head, like a deflated acorn. He removed that hat and hung it upon a hook in the entryway, revealing a head of chestnut brown hair, neatly parted despite the frayed disorder of all else he wore.

He was young, younger than any of those men who had come here before. He was nearly the same age as I had been, perhaps a few years older—twenty-five, I would guess. He bent over to set down his two cases upon the floor and nearly smiled as he stood back up, gazing at all the designs on the peeling wallpaper as though he found them fascinating. I was aware of my dissipated form gathering a little more in concentration of him, peering as closely as I could to study him, to understand. I suppose there are many things I have forgotten about being alive, such as how pupils dilate upon entering a darkened room, or the way throats twitch with a pulse. I brought my awareness that close to him—to witness the liquid sloshing through his veins, and how the follicles of his beard filled with new hairs to be shaved.

The first thing this man did was take a few eager strides toward the collapsed chaise lounge. He did not even bother to sweep off the layer of dust before attempting to sit down on it. He laughed at how far he sank into its peridot velvet cushions and how a cloud of dust exploded around him upon impact. If I could have laughed too, I would have. Humor is another concept imagined by the living; it has no bearing upon the Great Space but for the sound waves of laughter that rumble through matter.

The man seemed to want to stay in this house. After the chaise lounge, he explored every room by the faint daylight pouring in through the filmy, cracked windows. I had not even noticed the daylight.

If I wanted, I could dissipate from this concentration and have this all be irrelevant—yet another fleck lost in infinity—but I did not. I had not been so focused since they took everything from my home, leaving me with only broken pieces and the occasional mouse skittering against the wall. This man, whoever he was, I would remain concentrated for until he left. So I followed him closely. If only I knew how to communicate with him, I might ask him my questions . . .

A SONG BEYOND WALLS

Soon, he retrieved his cases and brought them up the stairs. There was still a desk before a window in my bedroom, and that was where he set them: right there upon the dust. I think he liked the view from the window and the flood of light that filled the room, because that's what I had liked so much about it, I remember. In this form, I cannot see out the window, as a great fog consumes my awareness beyond—I'm not sure why—but I remember there were many houses like mine separated by great trees, all set before the tall brick buildings of the city.

The man opened one of his cases and revealed within it a contraption I'd never before seen but remembered hearing about when I was living. It appeared to be a heavy box with lettered keys on it. The man loaded a piece of paper into it and twisted a knob until it fed through the machine. His long fingers went to the keys and began clicking away at them. I was fascinated that each letter as he pressed it appeared with a splatter of ink upon the page. I loved the clacking sound. I wished I had hands to touch it with. A word formed. Numbers. A date for a journal entry.

```
October 30, 1923
```

So... Twenty years into the new century. Thirty years since my unraveling.

He pressed more letter-keys, as swiftly and fluidly as one taps the keys of the piano. Sentences were forming; I was reading them as they poured from his fingers and onto the page. For the first time in these timeless decades I was anchored to a physical moment. Those keys as they pounded the paper swirled me, formed me, gathered me. I felt like I had shape. I *felt*.

```
 I have come to the house, at last, and
it is every bit as dusty and forlorn as
I had imagined it would be. Though every
inch of the house has been untouched
for decades, I cannot help but feel I
am in a stranger's home still.
```

The man paused from his work and sat back in the chair, reaching into his jacket pocket for a small matchbox and a cigarette. Cigarettes have much changed since my time. He struck a match and lit the end of the cigarette, sucking it to life.

His eyes found a candle upon the desk and, with the same flame, lit the wick after first wiping off the dust with his fingers. The light from the sun beyond the window was fading, and soon the entire house would be black, save the firelight.

He leaned forward again, and the words continued.

When he finished, he rose from the chair and stretched before crawling into the bed I once called my own. In the Great Space, dust is no different from any other matter, but when I was alive, I would have been appalled at his willingness to sprawl within it with no regard to his clothing. As he pulled back my moth-eaten coverlet, a cloud of dust filled the space and made him cough as he slipped beneath. He fell asleep quickly, exhausted—the breaths that filled his lungs slowing. I listened to them. I concentrated upon him so intently that I could feel the fabric of his sleep build within his subconscious. I was curious as to what I might see there.

In life, I remember stepping into the ocean and feeling the water rise from my feet to my ankles; that's quite what it was like permeating his subconscious. For an instant I felt flooded by his memories of sooty, sweaty work and the loneliness of lying upon an uncomfortable iron-framed bed among dozens. I saw trains rushing by on railroads, a rhythm of pickaxes striking rock, drills dipping into the earth, and factories spewing clouds of black.

In that same instant I waded into him, he gasped awake and choked on the dusty air.

He bolted upright in the bed; eyes wide open—green-brown eyes, searching the surrounding walls as though expecting to see someone standing before them. His mouth quivered with the urge to speak out, to call for someone, but his mind seemed to rule out that anyone could be there.

There was a consideration that there could be something *else* in the room, something he couldn't see, but I saw him shake his head of that notion and slip back down beneath the covers, consoling himself against fear.

He slept again. I did not disturb his dreams, but lingered around him like a cloud for what might have been hours of his life. I concentrated my particles then toward his letter-machine—I could not remember the proper name for it, even in life. I had no arms, not even phantasmal arms with which to reach for the keys. Smooth and hard, I imagined them to be, pressed against flesh fingertips. *Perhaps if I concentrate myself enough, as I have in these moments with this man, I may form something like that of limbs which I can stretch and touch with,* I reasoned.

The more I collected myself into a shape, the less I felt of the Great Space around me. But I soon had a figure. A human's figure . . . a *woman's* figure such as I had before, with arms and hands and fingers that I instantly reached out with to touch the letter-machine. But my fingers went through the keys like air, even still.

This concentration of my entirety—surely, other forms like mine have done similarly. How else are there tales of ghosts? But what was it, I wondered, which collected my unraveled particles all the tighter? Was it my mere will? Or could it have been his growing awareness of my existence? Perhaps it was both at once.

Now, as I moved about the house, I was not a dissipated entity, but a floating collection of shape. I thought I might have enough mass to make the candle in the bedroom flicker, just the slightest amount, if I passed by quickly enough. This, I tried over and over again. My effect upon the candleflame was measurable by decimals, but measurable nonetheless.

By the time the man awoke, I had collected myself into a form that was nearly human. As I swept through halls and floated down the stairway, the skirts of a phantasmal gown—the very image of the one I wore most in life—fluttered behind me; though for how much I reached for the railing in the hopes to slide my palm down it as I used to, I could never leave a streak of contact upon the dust.

When he came down the stairs, a little bleary-eyed but well-rested after a night of vivid dreams, I was collected in the parlor, trying again and again to force my fingers upon the keys of my old piano, but no matter how mightily I concentrated my form, I couldn't enter the physical world. And he still could not see me as he came into the room.

The first thing he did was part every torn, filthy pair of curtains to reveal the daylight beyond, illuminating the storms of dust swirling in the sunshine. I could perceive this detail much more clearly as though I had two eyes again, when before—when I was dissipated—a shine of light upon the broken table was lost in the Great Space. I could nearly sense heat, or at least I could remember the sensation of it.

As he walked by, he sighted the piano for the first time. Did he know how to play it? Oh, to experience the sound again—even if not through ears—but through reverberations of the walls and floor would evoke my human joy. What songs would he know, I wondered, in his time of this world? This 1923. Would he know Bach? Beethoven?

He came to stand before the piano just where my form was standing. He placed his hands where my hands were placed, and he began to press the keys so that it looked like mine were playing: *Moonlight Sonata*, a song I had learned as a child and knew still.

Never had I thought the Great Space could be shared between the confined living and the Rest, but I supposed there are some things that transcend the barrier. This was one of those instances. I felt a surge of life when he filled the house with music, shimmering and vibrating with every note, though wretchedly out-of-tune—and I think he might have felt elevated beyond life, unraveled a bit, because when he finished the song, he turned away and wiped at his eyes.

I followed him as he left the parlor and went to the front door. He slipped his hat from off its hook and secured it over the bed-tossed mess that was his hair and left through the door, leaving me on the other side of the barrier, vibrating still with the reverberations of our song.

The barrier between him and me—the one that had been permeated by our musical moment—I was now keenly aware of it. Like a bubble in the Great Space, the barrier protects the orderliness of the physical world from the disruption of infinite energies like myself . . . but I could feel the wall between us giving way the more I pressed against it.

Has this barrier always been so pliant? I wondered. I could not remember it being so when I had been desperate to reach for the living before. Could it be that I was stronger now than I had been then? Or perhaps it was the barrier which had weakened. I remembered reading of times when this was said to be possible: Samhain, Day of the Dead. Could it be mere coincidence that today, this All Hallow's Eve, was the very same day as those?

A SONG BEYOND WALLS

I looked down at my hands, vainly clasping a handle of the door, and saw that they had become more detailed with outlines of fingernails and etches of knuckles. My gown was more than an idea, but a memory: its lace and ribbons textured. I wondered what my face looked like now. I wished I could see my reflection in a mirror. Few things I'd forgotten about my life, and my own face was one of them.

The Flesh

My fingers trembled as I reached for a cigarette. *What is coming over me?* I felt like a tossing ocean. Unable to rest, unable to be still. And so many unnamed emotions, I could cry. I *did* cry. My lashes were still moist; my lips quaking so terribly, my cigarette dared to fall to the ground as I tried to light it. I had to get out of the house. I wasn't sure why, but it was just too much.

The strange thing was that I hadn't cried in years. And I had nothing to even cry *about*. What was it about playing that song that made me feel overpowered by every shining joy I've ever had? The first snow of winter . . . a wooden train for Christmas . . . splashing in the creek and catching tadpoles as a boy. Every human happiness filled me at once, and I nearly burst. I felt I could die with it—like that too-intense, tickling exhilaration you get when you're on a rollercoaster, stretched almost beyond capacity. But of all things I was doing, I was playing the piano. Like I'd done my entire life.

I had to admit . . . there *was* something about that house. I felt it the instant I walked in. Of course I'd heard the rumors, the ghost stories, but what I felt was nothing like what had been said. Sure, it felt like someone was watching me, but there was also this encompassing feeling of acceptance and . . . of perhaps . . . *love?* But that could have been my own love for the place resonating back at me. In a house that had been abandoned for that long, I imagined it was eager to absorb any emotions projected into it.

Still, that didn't explain why I awoke last night to the feeling of someone . . . or some *thing* . . . smothering me with their presence. But I have never been one to draw conclusions on the ambiguous. So much of this world we humans should never claim to understand or know.

All I *did* know was that the sun was warm, the air was fresh, and I was happy . . . for the first time, truly, in so long . . . or perhaps ever. So happy that I cried and could have cried still. I was home . . . *at last!* My first true home with its tattered curtains and peeling wallpaper. I had come so far to stand before the great emerald door with its eagle knocker, just as I had seen in the paper all those years ago. And one day I would invite everyone I could find from the asylum and show them that I—a penniless orphan—did it, as any one of us could. I bought the house I fell in love with as a child.

And now what would I do? So many have asked me that. What is a lone man to do in a grand old house where nothing works? Well, I was going to live in it. Yes, I would dust off the mantels and have the chimneys swept, patch up the walls and repair the plumbing . . . but I was in no hurry. To be honest, I quite liked the dust. Dust was the house's memory, and I wanted to know every inch of it.

A Collection

The man—oh how I wish I knew his name—was gone for hours. I could discern hours now.

When he returned, after hanging up his hat and setting shopping bags on the hall stand, he made a pointed glance toward where I was seated in the drawing room, as though he had sensed me there. Perhaps he was able to glimpse me out of the corner of his eye. But when he did a double-take, what image he had seen of me was gone.

He blinked in confusion, returned his focus to the front hall where he lit a three-arm candelabra, then carried a candle with him as he walked through the drawing and dining rooms on his way to the kitchen, defying the darkening evening with bouncing golden light.

In the kitchen he managed to get the old stove to light up, and in a pot he'd purchased he cooked himself dinner on it. I'd never seen anything like what he'd brought home: stew in a can. I thought it looked monstrous, but the more I watched him stir, the more appetizing it became. I was recalling all the flavors I loved when I was alive. How I loved the tastes of food, the satisfaction. Cakes and hams and berries and hot chocolate. I wondered if this man would ever bring any of my favorite foods here.

He ate by candlelight at a small table in the front hall, as the dining table had been one of the first things taken from the house. So badly I wanted to ask him his name and what he'd done all day.

He kept glancing in my direction. Uneasily, as though he could sense that I was standing there watching him, he cleared his throat. He seemed much distracted from his spoon, like he might speak to me at any moment. I waited eagerly for him to, but he never made another sound. Impatiently, I waved a hand over one of the three candles—*just* one of them, with more precision than any living being could hope to have—making the flame bend and writhe and nearly extinguish.

That got his attention. Slowly, he set down his spoon and looked around for me, but still I was unseen by him.

"Hello?" he asked of the room, uncertainty like gravel in his voice. I quite liked his voice. It was mellow . . . pleasant . . . patient.

I produced my greatest gust over the candle this time, ensuring the flame went out. Immediately he stood from his chair and stumbled back over it. There was at first an expression of terror on his face, but as he got to his feet—glancing about the room, noting the stillness and that the other two candles burned without a flicker to their flame—he laughed to himself nervously.

"Just a candle," I heard him murmur, "Doesn't mean anything."

Is that so? I thought, then sent a gust over the next candle so that it extinguished.

The man stood in awe of the two wicks that now swirled with smoke. He swallowed hard.

"I-I apologize . . ." he began timidly, but with a voice that carried through the house. "Clearly there is something . . . or some*one* here with me. I-is that right?"

I made the flame of the final candle flicker, but not go out.

He swallowed again.

"Well it is . . . l-lovely . . . to meet you," he said, and just after that, without a thought about it, he sprinted to the front door, threw it open, and was gone.

I hadn't meant to frighten him . . . However, when I thought about it from the living's point of view, I supposed I could have been more subtle. But then again, how does one commune between worlds subtly?

A Rapidly Beating Heart

If anyone had been watching me, they would have seen a grown man sprinting out the front doors of a dilapidated old house and likely have been able to assume the reason for my flight.

And on Halloween, of all nights.

However, I did not run far. I stopped as soon as my conscience began to reason with my fear. Yes, there was a spirit—a ghost—*something* in that house, and yes, it was terrifying, but I would have been lying if I'd said it felt like a hostile one. Even as I felt a gust of a presence moving past me to unsettle the flame, I felt nothing but affection in it. And the truth of the matter was that this spirit, this *thing*, had simply been attempting to communicate with me.

When I said 'hello', it answered back. When I asked a question, it replied. And now I felt like a cruel coward for fleeing from it.

Still, my fingers trembled as I lit another cigarette. Two times today I'd fled the house and jittered like a lapdog. For good reason though, I suppose.

With an exhale, smoke curled up into the night sky, cold and starry. I knew I had to go back inside, but I just couldn't force my feet to move.

Ultimately, I trudged back the way I came, as slowly as I could. Even the world outside was an eerie reminder of what awaited me in the house: Jack O' Lanterns on neighbors' porches leering at me in the dark and gauzy sheet-ghosts hanging from the old maple trees. I doubted these neighbors of mine had ever encountered a true ghost; for if they had, I was sure they would not have celebrated them in such a tawdry manner. And where did the idea to use sheets come from, anyway? Though I hadn't necessarily sighted the ghost, myself, I knew it didn't look like *that*. But there was an image in my head, which might have been purely imagination, of something far more graceful and elegant . . . more like how an angel might look.

By the time I reached the front doors, I had calmed from my jitters by reassuring myself that if the ghost wanted to hurt me, it would have already done so. The door squealed as I pushed it open. Still there was the bouncing light of the final candle—it wavered a little when the breeze of outside touched it, but that was all. Slowly, I walked inside, reluctantly closed the door at my back, and faced the entirety of the dark house before me, shivering in the shadows. *Was the ghost still here?*

A SONG BEYOND WALLS

"Hello again," I called out as kindly as I could, though my voice trembled a little. "I'm back. Sorry to have left in such a, uh . . . in such a hurry."

I cleared my throat. *Silence.*

Nervously, I combed my fingers through my hair. God, my hair was messy. *Are ghosts able to tell how your hair looks?* I wondered—angry with myself for such a stupid question.

A creaking sound . . . yes, I'd heard it. There was a creaking sound coming from the stairs, almost like someone was walking down them. I put my hand on the wall to keep myself from falling over. My blood felt like ice water rushing through me. *So much for not trembling.* I reached into my pocket for my handkerchief and dabbed at my forehead. *Just don't run out the door again, whatever you do. This is your house now, too. You're going to have to befriend this thing, and by doing so, you must have manners.*

"I hope I, uh . . . didn't offend you."

The spirit had creaked to the bottom stair. I could see that the railing had been smeared of its dust, like whomever descended did so with a hand upon it. I imagined a proper Victorian lady and felt a little relieved, but there was no way of knowing what or who the thing was. But now it was coming into the hall toward me.

I took an unintentional step backward, but the footsteps creaked off into the parlor. There was no light in there, so I grabbed the candelabra with its single flame and carried it in. *I must be crazy, following this thing,* I thought. How strange it was, though, that I felt familiar with it already. I wished I could have seen what it looked like...*if* there was anything to see. I wondered whether ghosts had a shape.

The bench of the piano creaked. I felt my mouth fall open, knowing what was about to happen but unable to believe it, unable to prepare myself. Tingles washed through me.

A very off-tune middle C rang in the silence. There was a long pause after it, as though this spirit was reveling in the long-carrying sound, almost like a test to see if it worked. And then without warning, *Fantaisie Impromptu* began to trill from the piano—as quick and masterful as a song right out of the phonograph, but more melancholy with the loose strings resonating like a long-lingering lament. I nearly swooned at the impossible sight of the piano keys moving by invisible fingers.

I'm dreaming. This is a dream.

And yet I knew I was very much awake . . . more awake than I had ever been in my life. Fear had frozen me cold, but my heart was boiling hot and pounding so rampantly, I feared it would burst through my chest. Never had I been so focused upon something; the way I watched those keys sink and rise was as though my very life depended on it.

When the song ended, my mouth opened to speak but all words had left me. I realized I was shaking again—the worst I'd shaken yet. Finally, a string of words impetuously escaped with my breath: *"Wh-who are you?"* they said; I hadn't even thought to ask it.

A SONG BEYOND WALLS

There was a pause long enough for me to think I would not get an answer. And how would a ghost answer such a question? But another song began to play. A song I knew. A simple nursery song I had loved and learned as a child: *Au Clair de la Lune*.

"Your name . . . your name is Claire!" I remarked with a tremulous smile.

The spirit jingled the highest keys in affirmation. *Claire,* I thought fondly. *So she is a lady.*

Every encounter I'd had with the spirit Claire returned to me with renewed understanding. The dream I woke so abruptly from last night; the astounding emotion felt when playing *Moonlight Sonata* earlier; the playful game with the candles; the feminine descent from the stairs. *Claire.*

My shaking relented as my body thawed of its fear, and my thoughts began to return to me.

So many things I wanted to say . . . so many questions to ask of her. Yet, again, I was speechless.

Feminine Phantom

He was simply standing there, a little dumbfounded. His hair still a mess, but it suited him better that way, I thought.

So now you know my name, I wanted to say to him. *What is yours?*

But I could not so easily ask him that by flickering a candleflame. I knew no titles of music I could play that would bear my questions.

I turned around on the bench and considered my options, glancing about the parlor. The table I had earlier admired the glint of sunlight upon had not yet been smeared of its furry layer of dust like many other surfaces had been in my musical friend's exploration of the house. All my many questions I had for him could not be written in so limited a space. So I glided over to it, extended a finger, and scrawled upon the smooth surface, *"Come Upstairs"*.

His eyes widened in horror, and he stared for a long time at those words before finally following my creaking ascent to the second floor. The candelabra trembled slightly in his grip as he walked behind me into the bedroom; there, I glided in and seated myself before his letter-machine.

I was so eager to touch the letter-keys; to imprint my intent upon the physical world in ways more permanent than the temporary—though ceaseless in the Great Space—reverberation of piano song. And finally, when I found my letters of choice and pressed my fingers upon them, that satisfying *clack* was proof of my existence; the splattering of ink on the paper my most physical image, far bolder than a slippery mark upon dust. My letters were:

```
What is your name?
```

Still, that dumbfounded expression hung on his face. He stood behind my chair with his mouth open, reading over the words as though translating them. Finally, his slackened mouth raised into an awed smile as he perhaps reconciled himself with the truth that I was so obviously communicating with him. He started to laugh. He covered his mouth to try to stop himself. He cleared his throat again and removed his hand to his side.

"Dorian." The smile crept into his voice and soon again his mouth. I had an inkling he'd never enjoyed saying his name so much before. "It's Dorian."

I felt the collection that made up my face rise with a smile. My phantasmal fingers returned to the keys. I knew how to operate the machinery by having watched my friend for so long the previous night. I was not as quick as he, but proudly I *clack*ed:

```
Hello, Dorian. Welcome.
```

Dorian looked as though his legs were weakening; he walked backwards until he caught himself on the bed and sat down. He stared off at where I was seated, clearly trying to make out some glimpse of me, then buried his face in his hands, massaging his closed eyes with fingers, kneading his forehead.

"Claire, I feel like I'm imagining this," he said wearily, "I'm afraid I'm going crazy, and that I'll wake up tomorrow disappointed that this was a hallucination. I want this to be real, I really do."

I continued to *clack* letters:

```
When you wake in the morning, this
paper with my words will still be here.
```

Dorian crept toward me again to peer at the words I had *clack*ed; he smiled generously. His smile made me remember that sensation of heat again. Hot sunny summer days. A fire rumbling in the hearth. Where my insides had once been, and my cheeks, is where I imagined that heat rising.

A SONG BEYOND WALLS

"Claire..." he started, then trailed off with a painful wince. "I have so many questions."

```
As do I.
```

"Who are you? I mean more than your name. Did you live here? Did you . . . *die* here?"

```
I did live here, and I still do. I
have lived here all my life. Until,
of course...I fell ill. It's a rather
long story and not a merry one.
```

"S-surely you want to tell it. After all these years."

There was silence between us as I considered, then the *clack*ing from my unseen fingers continued:

```
My father died of fever when I was
young. Since his death, my mother feared
sickness above all things...treating
me as if I was sick, too, for many
years, though I never was.

She never let me outside, and if I
ever was sick, that is why. I stayed
here in this house and played my piano
day after day. I had few visitors, but
my mother had many. When I was twenty-
```

```
two, my mother had been called upon by
a gentleman who was much travelled. He
must have carried with him some foreign
illness, and with my low tolerance for
illness, having seldom left the house,
I caught it and suffered much. All I
know after that is that my mother wept,
but soon left our home with the promise
of marrying that man. She took most
everything from the house but left the
memory of me. I have been this ever
since. Until you came here, I hadn't
known how long that was.
```

Dorian took a deep breath and looked toward where my face might have been, but his gaze fell when his eyes found nothing to latch to.

"Claire . . . I'm very sorry for you."

```
Now I want to know about you. Why
did you come here? Why do you like
the dust?
```

He chuckled.

"When I was a boy, I always dreamed of having a house of my own. 'Home' is a concept I'd never really known. Both my parents died before I was six, and ever since I have lived between relatives and ultimately the orphan's asylum.

A SONG BEYOND WALLS

"There were few joys when I was young: the first was my dream of having a home, the second was the piano in the asylum I learned to play, and played as much as I could. The rest of my joys fell into place whenever I had them: a Christmas present here, a trip to the river there. Nothing quite inspired me, however, until I found a discarded newspaper and saw a photograph of this very house with an article about how long it had gone without an owner, though several people had attempted to purchase it. I saved that article with the photograph and read it over every night in bed. I realize now that I saw my own identity in this house without an owner; the house of so much unrealized potential. I felt sorry for it as I felt sorry for myself. And I vowed then that I would be the one to own it. I would work hard and ultimately *that* house, the beautiful one with the eagle knocker on its emerald-green front door, would be my home.

"So that is what I did. I left the asylum to begin working at a very young age, grueling work—sometimes until I collapsed—and it has all been worth it because I'm now here, standing in the very house I vowed to live in, surrounded by the dust I have always dreamed of having smeared across my clothes . . . and talking with you, *Claire*, the very spirit of it all . . ."

He broke off. It seemed he had begun to feel as if he was going mad again. He considered it a moment, glancing back at the paper with my letters to remind himself that this was reality, and peering out of his periphery at where he imagined me to be sitting in the chair . . . wondering if perhaps I was really there, listening, and that he was not merely speaking this all into thin air.

> I'm here, Dorian.

He swallowed hard.

"How?" his voice was faint. "You were not here, not like *this*, just yesterday. Not even moments ago were you this real. I feel like every second you become more palpable to me, and it's more than just my perception of you. You're like the moon waxing into sight."

> I don't know how, exactly. Only that I was aware of everything and nothing before you arrived, and it is my fascination for you which has anchored me into this form. Perhaps, conveniently, the wall between our worlds has thinned as well and has allowed us to make contact . . . however brief this window may be. So much I have raveled since yesterday, and I feel I can ravel still, though how far I can go, I am unsure.

Dorian

Last night, Claire and I spoke and typed together until the light coming through the window lightened to gray, then gold. My eyelids were fluttering closed as I shared with her my every opinion and belief, and she shared with me her astounding descriptions of the infinite Great Space, until finally she suggested I get some sleep.

I was aware of very little as I made my way to the bed: the brightness of the room, how the papers she had typed littered the floor, and how I felt buoyant upon water that rippled, threatening to submerge me in a dream. As I collapsed upon the dusty covers and fought against the heaviness of my eyelids—my gaze still fixed upon where I had known her to be—I could have sworn I saw her at last: translucent but framed by glimmering sunlight, rising from the chair and walking so delicately over to the bedside.

The silhouette of a high-necked gown with puffed sleeves, of long hair.

I hated myself for my inability to keep my eyes open. I wanted so desperately to look upon her, to take in her features, but sleep was consuming me like the ocean's inevitable waves. My buoyancy was nothing in comparison.

"Please be here when I wake up," I slurred with a foolish smile—then I'm sure I snored.

When I jolted awake a few hours later, it was with the panic that Claire had been only a dream. The bedroom, sobered with crisp autumn daylight, seemed worlds away from my visions of flickering candleflames and pianos that played themselves. As I wiped the sleep from my eyes, I shook my head of its madness—of this grief I felt for a lady I had so perfectly dreamed of—who had felt to me of bright snow and rich raspberry cake. *Had I truly only slept so little,* I wondered, *when it seemed like years I was away with her?*

"Claire," I said to myself, my heavy head held in my hands. I did not want to go and look at the typewriter to see I had only dreamed of her words. The disappointment would be too much.

Then I heard it: the first prelude of *The Well-Tempered Clavier* playing from the piano downstairs, and I scampered like a clumsy puppy out of the room, down the stairs, and into the parlor. And what I saw before me made me freeze up and stop in my tracks: a fully-visible woman seated upon the bench before the piano, properly poised in a wine-colored gown from an era before I was born, with hair the color of honey curling down to the middle of her back.

"Claire . . ." I whispered.

She stopped playing. She turned her face to me. I saw her face. Her smile.

"Dorian." Her voice . . . a bell tolling in the sunshine, ringing and bright. She stood from the bench and stepped out around it.

How did I think myself capable of imagining her?

I could not stop myself from running across the parlor to her. I didn't know what to do, so I just stood as close as gentlemanly possible before her, studying her face as she looked up at me.

She was as pale as one could be for having never left the house, and still she was shimmering with translucence as I had seen in the dawn light this morning, making her look luminous as a polished pearl, while little more substantial than a cloud. And so slight-of-body she was, I thought that if indeed she was tangible enough, I could easily pick her up and hold her, and oh, how I wanted to.

Her eyes as they looked up into mine were heavy and dark for being hazel, and she had the same interested, dessert-rich gaze I'd imagined her to have had all this time.

I was not certain whether I would be able to touch her if I reached for her hand to kiss . . . but I attempted it all the same. I bent over and extended my hand for hers—she gave it to me. And yes, I could feel it, the light little thing. More than a cloud, indeed. I closed my fingers around her and felt the perimeter of her existence. It was a faint line, still, and I likely could have crushed my fingers through her and into the air, but I dared not exert more than the gentlest force. My kiss was even gentler.

Claire

I felt myself become more substantial just since Dorian woke. His attention to me might have been a great part of my collecting into this lifelike form, but the even greater part was my own desire to experience life again. I wondered how long I could stay this way, how human I could become, but I preferred not to think about it just then. There were too many things to enjoy for me to be distracting myself with limitations.

My first thought when Dorian touched me was how warm he was. I could feel it . . . warmth. And his kiss evoked tingling sensations in my hand that made me want to yelp out with excitement. But all I did was smile . . . smile serenely at him. We looked at each other without speaking for a very long while, until finally, he broke the silence.

"I've wanted so badly to see you, and yet . . ." he broke off, thinking of the words. "I feel I've seen you before. In my heart I saw you just as vividly as I am seeing you now."

At his words, his praise, I was aware of my flesh becoming more opaque; my hand in his becoming more substantial. The velvet of my gown, however, was still just a memory—a figment of my subconscious—and would not permeate the physical world as I could . . . however I was doing it.

Quickly, I retracted my hand from his and covered my chest with my arm. My other hand went to the place beneath my navel.

"I need clothes! *Hurry!*"

Dorian quirked a brow at me, and, seeing my arm crossed before my bosom—and perhaps the first outlines of my fleshly figure emerging from beneath the fading velvet—blushed like a tomato before clumsily hurrying out of the parlor. I heard a jingling of keys, the sound of him taking his hat off the hook, and then the closing of the front door.

The fabric of my gown continued to grow more translucent until it disappeared completely, and I was left with naught but my flesh, nearly as opaque as any living human's, albeit with still a glow that shimmered almost iridescently.

As I went about each window to close the curtains with care, I relished in every touch and sensation of my skin against the material world. I had even begun to laugh with joy . . . and I had found such pleasure in laughing, the resonant booms echoing from out of my very heart and into the surrounding Great Space, that I laughed all the more. I began to sing too. I spun about the dark curtain-drawn house, naked but glowing, singing every song I loved most and rejoicing in how they felt vibrating through me.

If only I had enjoyed this world more when I was alive. I should have yelled and pranced and ran out the house without regard to what I was told. But oh, to have the chance to experience it again . . . even for a moment! I don't understand how it's possible, but I shan't waste a second of it.

I had been anticipating Dorian's return, and so by the time I heard the door squeal open, I had confined my nakedness to my dressing room. He called out for me and, when I answered, handed me three shopping bags through a crack in the door.

"I did the best I could," he offered. "I had to guess on the shoe size. Everything else should fit . . . for the most part."

I unpacked the first bag and unwrapped a pair of stockings and some silk undergarments I had never seen before, but could easily imagine which parts of the body they were assigned to. I expected these insubstantialities to be worn underneath a whalebone corset and petticoat, but to my surprise there were no other such undergarments. I had begun to hope Dorian had made a mistake by forgetting such necessities, but when I saw the dress—if such a simple thing could be considered a dress—I knew no mistake was made.

"Does it simply go over your head?" I asked in awe.

"I suppose," I heard his nervous voice from the other side of the door. The poor man had just about as much a clue about this dress as I did. And oh, how bizarre this must have been for him.

"This is what ladies wear now, is it?" I tried not to sound condescending, but *really*, where had the fashion gone? In my lifetime, dressing was an extravagant discipline. But this? To simply slip a dress over my head? What would my mother say?

After I'd done it, I realized the genius of it. It was quite liberating to dress so easily. However, I felt very much exposed with the length of the dress so short that the hem revealed my shins. I wondered what happened in the last thirty years to reverse centuries of modesty. Thankfully, the women today still had enough sense to wear stockings, but I would not be surprised if that was a modesty lost soon as well.

"How does it fit?" he asked.

"Is it supposed to be so loose? There's no waist!"

"Compared to the gown I'd just seen you in, yes, very much so."

I unwrapped the contents of the next bag and found a box containing shoes. Now these were a little more to my taste, but still very strange. They were a heel with a single strap extending across the top of the foot. I wobbled my feet into them, then unwrapped the contents of the final bag, curious what other article was vital to the women of this era. It was a hat . . . of a unique shape: very bowlish, almost like a bonnet. I put it on, then opened the door. His uncertain expression suddenly brightened with a smile.

"I did well!" he remarked. "I should have bought you beads and gloves too. That would have been absolutely perfect."

I looked down at the swish of the dress against my legs, my feet in the shoes. Was I really here? In a time other than my own?

"It must be overwhelming for you," he said, clearly taking my wistfulness for dissatisfaction. "To be back in this world and have it be so different. I'm sorry, I would have found a gown more suitable to what you're used to, if only I—"

"It's wonderful!" I interjected, smiling at him. I had to lift my chin higher to meet his eyes with the brim of the hat so low. "And I'm really not upset. Not at all. Why would I be, when even the sound of my own voice is a miracle. I want to see, do, and *feel* all there is!"

"Then would you . . ." he began, leaning against the wall to appear all the more coolly composed, when really, it was not difficult for me to tell he was ill with his nervousness. "Maybe . . . want to leave the house with me . . . for a while?"

I blinked, considering the possibility. "I-if I could ... I would want nothing more."

He extended his hand for me to take. "Shall we try?"

My mind was whirring with the imagery of nature, blooming and bursting. Plants and water and weather. Distractedly, I took his hand and together we descended the stairs to the front door.

I swallowed uneasily when I stood before it.

"I'm afraid," I admitted. "Fear is something I have not felt since I unraveled. Part of my fear is that—if I face the white fog beyond the threshold—I might unravel again."

"I understand." He gripped my hand tighter. "We don't have to, of course."

I thought about the timeless void in which I had been existing: a stationary cloud unable to move from the confines of the house I could never leave, even when I was alive. And yet here I was now, before the exit, with a substantial hand that could grip the door handle and turn it. A hand within the physical world.

"There is no reason I should not try," I argued against my trepidation, and slowly reached a hand for the handle. The metal was cold against my firming flesh. I turned it, and pulled.

Blinding white light beyond the door made me clamp my eyes closed. I let out a scream, expecting my particles to dissolve and for all reality to shatter like a mirror all over again—but Dorian held me. I was still here.

The door squealed open. I opened my eyes.

Living

I'll never forget the way Claire looked at the world beyond the front doors. I'd supposed if a newborn baby had the knowledge of what things were when they were born, that might look similarly. The afternoon sunshine was so bright in her smarting eyes, but she wouldn't let them close, not even for a blink, because she dared not lose a precious moment of vision.

I was glad for her that the sun was out and that the day was a mild one. She would not even need a coat. And the grass was still green, and the flowers still in bloom despite the roaring red leaves of autumn in the trees all around us. All seemed calm, but to her, I'm sure it was a symphony of senses. When a car roared by, she darted back into my arms with a gasp.

"What *was* that?"

I chuckled. "A car. There are a lot of things like that now. You won't see many horse-drawn vehicles anymore. Not here in the city, at least."

A SONG BEYOND WALLS

"I remember... *sensing*... that technology's changed, but seeing it? Unbelievable."

I realized I was staring at her quite like how she was staring at the things around her. This lovely young woman who was a spirit-turned-corporeal. *Unbelievable, indeed,* I thought ironically.

For those hours we were out of the house together, I simply watched her as she explored, and if there was some place she wanted to go, I jumped eagerly at the opportunity to guide her there. Her wonder was inexhaustible, as even the ants on the pavement and the smell of motor oil made her—and me—stop to appreciate the wonder of them.

It was those smaller, easily dismissible details which held her attention the most. Through them, I learned that often it was these things, rather than the seemingly superior ones, which would be most sorely missed from life. As she gazed up at the fiery red maple trees, I waited for her to ask about the dreadful sheet-ghosts which hung from them—who ostensibly mocked her—but she was too engrossed in the commotion of birds upon the boughs to care. And that was another lesson I learned from her. Nothing could distract her from the beauty of this living, breathing world.

I knew she was very much human when she said that she was hungry. She sniffed the air and followed her nose into a diner. She ordered a hamburger, and I held back laughter as I watched her figure out how to eat it without compromising her etiquette. After much protesting, she used a fork and knife, carving away at the burger daintily, and I finally allowed myself to laugh. She laughed, too.

How could it be that I loved her already?

I bought us both a soda pop to share because she saw a couple at another table drinking one. I warned her of the carbonation—that it's an acquired sensation. At first her eyes burned and she coughed, but she enjoyed the "million little explosions" of the bubbles going down her throat. I certainly hadn't thought of it that way before.

"Unraveling is quite like an explosion," she began to explain, dabbing at her eyes with a napkin. "I suppose it's rather like a star dying. A supernova. And all your matter—even your thoughts and memories—explode into the Great Space, and you become a cloud of scattered matter . . . like a nebula.

"It's so difficult to come together again," she continued. "Especially when there is nothing in the physical world to hold onto: no one saying your name, no one paying a visit, nothing left behind for you . . . not even a glove you had once worn. The concentration of my collectedness was parallel to the connections I had with the physical world. And before you, I had only a house I could not leave and a piano I could not play . . . so I was spread out, unfocused, and for the most part, unaware of my loneliness."

"That might explain why you couldn't leave before," I suggested after a sip from my straw. "Most of your life was spent in the house. You hardly made connections with anything beyond . . . nothing to anchor you to it. Had you gone outside more, I wonder whether you could have maneuvered to the rest of the world."

We continued to talk of these mysteries as we wandered the city, linking arms and leaning our heads together. The more I held her, the stronger her body was against me, and I had difficulty believing she was ever invisible to me.

I paid for a taxi to drive us around, just so that she would latch onto me in the back seat and scream delightedly at the wind whistling through her hair. The driver, and all who we passed on the street, gawked at us as though we were escapees from a madhouse.

When she saw a flashing sign for 'music', she yelped for the taxi to stop, and we dove out into oncoming traffic, laughing despite the honking horns. She pulled me by the arm across the street and inside the building, where we found ourselves within a swarm of a jazz show.

She marveled at the musicians on stage and the wonderful amount of energy blasting from their instruments and from the crowd. After we danced together for hours, I promised her the cinema was perhaps the greatest invention in human history and led her there to watch a film. While it played, we crept to the back of the theater so that she could goggle at the projector.

It was night when we left the cinema, and cold. Clouds had consumed the moon, and a frigid moisture carried on the wind like it might rain. I slipped off my suit jacket and wrapped it snugly around her arms. She wanted to stay in my embrace as we walked.

"I have one memory of being outside the house when I was very young," she said to me. Her voice was quiet and contemplative for the first time in hours of roaring fun. "My father took me to the ocean. I wish I could go there again now . . . but it's days away and I don't know how long I'll be this way."

I felt myself prickle with a cold terror. I brought our walking to a halt. "You . . . you think you won't stay in this form?"

"I don't know." How heavy her dark eyes looked as she considered her fate. Those eyes looked up at me. "It doesn't feel stable, this body."

"But you said I've helped anchor you. And I'm not going anywhere."

Her somber expression lightened with a slight smile. I was only speaking the truth, but I suppose those words lifted her from an eternity of loneliness.

My mouth felt an irresistible gravitational pull down to hers and wanted more than anything to press against it, but it had begun to rain, and she began to laugh a true, hearty laugh.

"I can feel it!" she rejoiced as fine droplets splashed upon her face. "The ocean is in this rain." And she spun around as the rain fell even harder; holding out her upturned palms to receive it. "All the water . . . it's connected."

We were soaked when we came back to the house. I left the cab driver with an extra tip for us having drenched his back seats. I hurried to light a fire in the parlor and put flames to all the candles so we were not in total darkness.

"I thought of visiting my grave," Claire said as she stood before the fireplace. "But I decided against it. Why remind myself of what I already know?"

"What about your mother? Would you have visited her if she was still alive?"

"She is," said Claire without hesitation, taking the cloche off her head and setting it upon the mantle; her hair beneath damp and curled. "And no. Many things are worth our limited energy in this world, but we should not spend it on what will only continue to drain it away."

I had no idea what to say to that; Claire had rendered me speechless all the day long.

"It's interesting . . ." she continued. "There are some things which sap our energy, and others which grow it. You cannot observe this in the Great Space. Only in the physical world can emotions and art seemingly bend the laws of physics. Dance, music, love . . . these things take energy to produce, yet in doing so you're fulfilled with even more."

I crossed the room to her and leaned against the wall so that I could see her face. There were tears glistening with the firelight in her eyes, though her face was completely still and solemn.

"Claire . . ." I reached for her hand. When taking her flesh to mine, I noticed that it had become less substantial than before; that pearly glow of translucence having returned, I had not noticed it so keenly in the dark outside. A sharp intake of breath revealed to her my horror. "Y-you're fading . . ."

"I know," she whispered levelly, letting the tears stream down her cheeks. I imagined it was for the sensation, the warmth against her skin and the saltiness when the tears reached her lips, that she did not wipe them away. "Whatever has happened to me is reversing."

"Reversing?" I breathed with agony, realizing I now had tears building in my eyes. My jaws ached so badly, I had to clench my teeth together.

"It has nothing to do with my intent, for I want nothing more than to remain as I am," she began, her eyes still not having left the fire. "Had it not been for my intent, and your attention to me, I never would have collected into a form that has allowed me to travel here. But the doorway to the physical world had to be open to receive me, and receive me it did. But now the doorway is closing—and I am being pushed out, it seems. Like a boomerang circling back."

"Why?" I knew it was a foolish thing to moan out like a child; not a question for her to answer, but a plea against the inevitable—like the lost boy I had been in the orphan's asylum, deprived by death all over again. The tears in my eyes blurred the image of her coming into my arms, gathered tightly against my heart. I buried my face in her hair. Cradled the back of her head with my hand.

"That is the question, isn't it? 'Why'?" she reasoned, her voice muffled pitifully against my chest. "Why should any of this have happened at all, if it will only end?"

I took her chin gently upon my forefinger and lifted it so I could see her lovely, tear-streaked face. The thought of it disappearing from this world made my mouth twist and tremble.

"You know why," I argued—and sniffled. "It is because I love you, and you love me too, I think. And living or beyond, we have waited for this all our existence. And it will not end. We have all the Great Space and all of immeasurable Time to love each other, still."

I cannot recall if it was her or me who leaned for it first—I suppose it was both of us in perfect harmony—but our mouths melted together, and the rest of the night was a sweet, sweet dream.

I tried to stay awake all the night, so as not to miss a detail of her fading, but her body beside mine was such a comfort to me. She had been petting my hair and kissing my forehead, urging me to sleep like I was a tender child. I had the feeling she was trying to spare me the horrific sight of seeing her slowly vanish from this world.

"Please be here when I wake up," I said to her just as I had the previous night. I felt her face smile against mine—so faint now. She whispered that she will always be here. This was our home, after all.

In the morning, I blinked my eyes open and looked beside me upon the bed. I knew Claire was lying there, naked and pleasure-flushed, still, but I could not see her. Only the faintest sparkle of sunlight revealed her silhouette to me. Then, in moments, it was completely gone.

For hours I sat on the edge of the bed—my eyes raw, red, and staring. I waited to hear the piano play . . . a clack of the typewriter.

Nothing.

For the first few months after Claire's fading, I was torn between the madness of wondering whether I had imagined it all and whether it would ever happen again.

For days, the dress and undergarments I had bought her lay scattered upon the bedroom floor . . . evidence enough of her having been real . . . and yet, I still stared at them disbelievingly. I eventually packed them away into a closet, but I left the cloche upon the mantle in the parlor.

Each day I spent hard at work, eager to busy my mind so as not to lose it. I could have gone mad with all the speculations of what Claire may have endured when she disappeared from this world: if she had gotten lost; if she had been terrified; if it was painful for her to virtually die again; or if she was forever gone, dissipated beyond recollection.

In that time, I had restored the house enough for it to function like a comfortable home. I added another chaise lounge from Claire's time which I hoped she would approve of—should she ever return—and several other pieces of furniture, like a great long dining table and an oil lamp chandelier. I even had the piano polished and tuned. Still, it has not been played.

I did dream of her, however. Dreams so distant, I felt I had to squint my dream-eyes to perceive her. Dreams of her standing before an ocean, her wine-red gown rippling with the wind; dreams of her lost from me but more found by herself than she has ever been before.

A SONG BEYOND WALLS

Intangible, further from this world than my consciousness could reach, but always connected to me by a strand.

It took nearly a year to shake myself of the anxiety that I might never know what happened to Claire or if she would return. I found it easiest not to ponder such mysteries and simply relish in the spectacular experience that she and I briefly shared.

Loneliness was something I had gotten used to in my life, but after Claire's departure, the silence of it was too heavy. The only thing to alleviate that loneliness was discovering a small black kitten—an orphan like myself—mewing in a sewer pipe. Umbra, I named her: my little darling who slept between my chin and chest every night. I hoped, foolishly, that Claire would love her too when she returned.

But she hasn't returned yet, so she likely never will, I continually reminded myself—even as I purchased a well-preserved crimson velvet gown from 1891 that looked so much like the one Claire had donned in her subconscious—and hung it up in the dressing room with a note attached that read *'for when the barrier allows'*. I had even planned a special dinner for her upon Halloween night—the anniversary of our first encounter—as it came again, with all the foods I knew her to love best. Whether Claire came or not, I would cook the feast, tie a bow at my throat, and set the grand dining table for two. And now I had only to wait, allowing myself the slightest bit of hope that she would return to me.

Limitless

When my particles unraveled from the physical world, I collected myself again as soon as I was able—but I was not at home anymore. At first, all I could perceive was sound and motion . . . more energy than my vulnerable, newly collected form could fathom, roaring my particles and threatening to explode them apart at an instant. Then, once I became more concentrated, I realized I stood before the great, undulating collection that was the ocean.

The sun and the moon passed over the horizon, one after the other, a chase in a loop. So fast, at first, it was a blur of white and red. But then I remembered that I could either disregard the passing of Time and exist in a void of irrelevance, or anchor myself to any unit of it. For a while I enjoyed Time as slowly and languidly as a child—then I sped it up to the distracted haste of an adult. For a while, at least, I would perceive the physical world at Dorian's rate, but he would not be alive for eternity, and that's what I had. His entire life could pass before me as blurredly as the sun and the moon, but I wanted to exist in it with him slowly, moment by moment.

A SONG BEYOND WALLS

I wasn't sure how long I stayed at the ocean before I was able to anchor myself to Time, but after the anchoring, it was several sunsets and moonsets that I lingered there, feeling my particles sway with the rhythm. In and out, up and down, like waves with the moon.

How did I get here? I could not remember; my consciousness must have unraveled a little too much in the process. Last I could recall, I was lying beside Dorian in the bed, watching him sleep. I had thought I would have remained in the house when I unraveled, like I had the first time—but instead, I was here . . . limitless.

The Great Space was the same as it had been to me before, but now I was free in it; the moon as near to me as the end of my arm. I could reach for it, seize it, wrap myself around it. If I wanted, I could sink between the spaces of the atoms in the sun or take a ride on light. I could distance myself from the anchored moment, pull myself deeper into the Great Space, and view the tableau of it as something miniscule. I could see all the barriers of the physical world like rotating disks that thickened and thinned: all a machine, a clock, a loop like the sun chasing the moon over the horizon. And I could reel myself back in again.

The first time I unraveled, waves of sound and blasts of energy exploded me a million times until I gathered myself against them, forming an island in the tumultuous Great Space. But not this time. This time I had never dissipated too fully. Perhaps it was Dorian's love for me which was a beacon through the jostling matter, connecting me to life, even still. With it I could still feel emotions, if I wanted to; I could perceive the Great Space with the eyes and heart of the living. I was stronger, too. I felt so collected that if I were to unravel again, it would be less catastrophic to my entirety, and even less so after that.

How long had Dorian been awaiting me, I wondered. All this time—however long it was—he was likely waiting for a sign of me: a *clack* from the letter-machine, a *ding* from the piano, a smear of the dust, or a flicker of a flame. Had it been years? It could have been, but he was still alive, this I could feel in my connection to him. When my particles had gathered themselves to a strength I felt would hold against the tumult of the Great Space, I left the ocean for him. For our home.

I slipped in through the exterior wall into our bedroom. A rosy cast of evening light filled the space, and Dorian was nowhere to be found in it. All was still and silent.

I looked out the window. I could see beyond it! There was no blinding fog, but a clear view of the sleepy street, and the orange grimaces of Jack O' Lanterns upon my neighbors' porches.

I turned my glance back to the room. Since I had last been here, the dust had been wiped away, except for a few neatly squared patches which I could only assume had been an invitation for me to write upon. Even the mirror on the wall across from me was free of dust, yet I still could not see my reflection in it. I wondered, since I was invisible to the eye, whether I could make contact upon the physical world or not.

Tentatively I extended a finger to a furry patch of dust upon the windowsill. The slightest flakes stirred at my touch, and the more I willed myself to the physical world, the more matter I permeated. Soon there was a slight dimple, but too slight to be seen.

I turned to regard the rest of the bedroom, which was clean and bright in the autumnal glow, when my attention was seized by a pair of large, glassy, yellow eyes looking right at me.

A small black kitten had been curled up at the foot of the bed, but was now alertly looking at me, fluffy black tail flicking interestedly.

As a test to see that the kitten was truly aware of me and not a fly on the wall behind me, I moved across the room and its yellow eyes followed. I crossed back in the other direction and its eyes followed again. After seemingly deciding that I was of no threat to itself nor its home—or perhaps it was simply out of laziness—the kitten lowered its chin to the blanket and let its eyes fall closed.

My particles raised with a smile. *I've never had a pet before.*

I heard some clanking down in the kitchen below. The kitten opened its eyes apathetically at the sound with an ear turning toward the door.

"Could that be your father?" I asked the kitten, who only blinked at me before raising its hind legs and stretching shakily. After an enormous yawn, the kitten jumped off the bed and came strutting toward me, rubbing its side against my invisible legs. I bent down to scratch its head. "Let's go say hello to him, shall we?"

The kitten followed as I descended the stairs. Dorian had purposefully left a line of dust upon the railing, which my hand followed as I made my way down to him; more and more of the dust chafing off into the air as I became more raveled. How much older would Dorian be, I wondered. What would he look like now? It could not have been more than a year since I had left him. Though however long it was, he had done much to make it a gleaming, delightful home. And really, *gleaming*. I followed a bright flood of light coming from the dining room and saw that he had installed a magnificent chandelier that reflected upon a glossy oak table, which was set for two.

I walked around the perimeter of the table, nearly weeping with happiness at all I saw. Not only was there a steaming pot of hot chocolate and several dome-lidded platters and tureens that surely possessed delicious foods that I wished I could have smelled, there was also a bouquet of red roses upon a luscious velvet gown laid out upon the table. And not a flimsy excuse for a *dress*, but a true evening gown from my time. I stroked my hand across it. I could feel the fabric like a vibration against my gathering form, like a sweet song.

The door to the kitchen opened and in walked a tall, lean man dressed sharply in a fashion of my own era: a black tailcoat and pants striking against a white u-collar waistcoat and bowtie. The only cue that this was not some fashion-plate illustration of the perfect gentleman was the cigarette tucked behind his ear. *Dorian*: as young and beautiful as I had left him. And every particle of matter I possessed was rendered immovable at the sight of him.

A SONG BEYOND WALLS

He was carrying two crystal goblets in his gloved hands and set them in their proper places upon the table. I wondered if those goblets were to be the vessels for the hot chocolate. Oh, I wanted to laugh. Dorian ... precious Dorian. It was evident he could not see me as he made his way around the table, but as he came to where I stood, frozen in awe of him, he stopped too—just before me, his face so close to mine. His eyes widened, he breathed in slowly. I brought a hand to the side of his face and he closed his eyes at my touch.

"Claire?" he whispered with such torment. I recalled the sensation of scalding tears with clarity.

Yes, I answered him, but I had no voice with which to speak. So I reverted to the only other language the two of us spoke; I left the dining room for the parlor and sat at the piano.

Fulfilled

I told myself I would not give in to the slightest sensations that might indicate Claire's return; too many times have I done that already. Every pop and shift and wintry draft in the old house sent me running down the stairs, begging for her to speak to me. Could this be yet another of those times, or was it really her?

I could not so easily give in to the hope that she was, truly, right before me. I hoped it so many times, and it hadn't been real then. *But it feels real now.*

However, just as soon as I felt it—the fantasy of her—it was gone in a waft of raspberry-dessert-feeling air. I looked over my shoulder to the doorway leading into the drawing room and had the strongest urge to follow. It appeared I was not the only one lured to do so: little Umbra, with her fluffy tail poised confidently in the air, led the way before me. She strutted through the drawing room and front hall, and over to the piano bench in the parlor, rubbing her body against something, or someone, who was obviously there which I could not see.

Here, I stopped in my tracks and began trembling again. God, I hadn't trembled in a year. My mouth began to twist again; my eyes spilling with tears. I waited for the sound. My entire life depended on the sound.

C

STEPHANIE ESCOBAR was querying literary agents for her grandiose fantasy saga when she wrote *A Song Beyond Walls* as a side project. She had written it specifically for an anthology in the hopes of having it published . . . but that changed when her husband asked the pivotal question: "Why not publish it yourself?". Stephanie rose to the challenge, fell in love with the process, and plans to expand on the story in the future.

She lives with her husband and daughter in a misty forest town in Northern Idaho, where she runs a small homestead, bakes far too much, and hand-feeds gnats to her free-roaming spiders. She welcomes visitors to her site, sescobarauthor.com and to her social media platforms.

Made in the USA
Monee, IL
27 June 2023